Just Plain Bob

THE REDHEAD'S *Desires*

Hot Romance Erotica

About the Publisher

4Fun Publishing, a member of **BLVNP Incorporated**, 340 S. Lemon #6200, Walnut CA 91789, info@blvnp.com / legal@blvnp.com
NOTE: Due to the highly emotional reaction of some people to works of erotic fiction, any email sent to the above address that contains foul language or religious references is automatically deleted by our anti-spam software and will not be seen. All other communications are welcome.

DISCLAIMER

You want me on the desk, or bending over and leaning on it?"

Mary Jane loves her husband Peter so much but his deficient member can't keep up with her insatiable sexual appetite.

While Peter is busy with his two jobs as a superhero and a freelance photographer, Mary Jane busies herself, scouring the big city for part-time lovers who can satisfy her carnal needs.

When Kraven the Hunter gets pardoned and becomes a free man, Peter and Mary Jane are drawn unto him in the most mysterious circumstances. What happens next is the most exciting adventure that this superhero and his wife will get into…

The Redhead's Desires
Hot Romance Erotica

By: Just Plain Bob

ISBN: 978-1-68030-038-3

Chapter 1

It took a second to register, but when it did he reacted quickly. Rolling down the partition, he instructed the driver to pull over to the curb. As the limo pulled over, he turned to the short, balding man sitting next to him.

"I've found my female lead. See the redhead coming down the walk toward us? Find out everything about her that you can. She's the one. I knew it as soon as I saw her that she is the one."

"Why her?"

"Because as soon as I saw her, a voice in my head said, 'That one!' You know that I never ignore that voice. The last time I didn't listen to it I ended up in prison. You're wasting time; get out, follow her and find out everything that you can and report back to me as soon as possible."

It was twenty-four hours later when the short man gave his report. "Her name is Mary Jane Parker. She is twenty-seven, married and is an out of work model and an aspiring actress."

"She wants to be an actress, does she? Perfect, just perfect. I'll just have to see how bad she really wants to see her name in lights. What about the husband?"

"Peter Parker, a freelance photographer for The Daily Bugle."

"Freelance? That's French for he can't hold a job. Obviously, a man of no consequence. It should be fairly easy for me to make his wife my bitch."

Kraven The Hunter smiled his predatory smile as he envisioned the luscious redhead spread naked before him.

~~***~~

"What do you mean, 'pardoned?' How can they justify pardoning a hardened criminal?"

"That isn't your concern Parker. All you need to know is that he is out of prison and that I want pictures of him. He is news; news sells papers and in case you have forgotten, selling newspapers is what I do. Now get out of here and get me pictures."

As Peter Parker left the office, a silver-haired black man who had been sitting in a corner of the room said, "Why do you always antagonize that boy Jonah? He's a good kid and he gets you some great photos for the paper."

J. Jonah Jameson took the cigar out of his mouth and looked at the black man, "Think about it Robby. Give it thirty seconds and see if it comes to you."

Thirty seconds later Robby shook his head no. Jameson said, "I hack on him all the time every time he comes around and as a result he never comes here unless I call him in to give him an assignment. So, in a way, I control his comings and goings at The Bugle, right?"

"Yeah, but why is that important?"

"Think, Robby, think! If he stays away unless I call him he is less likely to find out that we are fucking his wife. You do want to keep sinking your black cock into her soft white body, don't you?"

"Hell yes I do."

"I know you do and so do I. By the way, she will be here at five-thirty. You have condoms?"

"In my desk drawer. I still don't think it's fair that you get to ride her bareback, but that I have to use rubbers."

"It isn't fair Robby, but it is necessary. If I knock her up as long as the kid doesn't come out with a brush cut and smoking a cigar we are all right. You knock her up and there would be hell to pay."

~~***~~

Peter Parker, also known as Spider-Man (although only to his wife), left The Daily Bugle Building with his hands in his pockets and a scowl on his face. One of these days, he thought, I'm going to shove that damn cigar so far down Jameson's throat that his ass will blow smoke rings when he farts. Just then his Spider Sense sent a tingle through his body and he looked up to see a limo driving by. The limo had smoked windows so he couldn't see inside, but the Spidey Sense told him it was Kraven The Hunter.

Peter still had a hard time believing that they had let Kraven out of prison, but out he was and Jameson wanted pictures. He flagged down a cab and when he got in he told the driver to, "follow that limousine." The driver, acting like he heard that all the time, pulled out into traffic and tagged along behind the car Peter had pointed out.

~~***~~

Mary Jane looked at her watch as she entered the Bugle Building, five-twenty, right on time. She had been looking forward to this all day. She hoped that Robby and Jonah had been taking vitamins. She smiled to herself as she thought about how she was going to wring them dry. It was a win/win situation for her. They thought she was bribing them to give Peter work and so they did keep him in assignments, which kept him out of her hair, but the real reason she was spreading her legs for them was that she was a cock hungry slut. They were just two more names on the long list of lovers that she needed just to keep her satisfied.

As she rode the elevator on the way up to Jameson's office she thought, and not for the first time, about that stupid fucking radioactive spider that had bitten Peter. Why in the hell couldn't that bite have done something for Peter's pee-pee. She giggled at that, it was so small that she couldn't even call it a dick. What good was it having all that strength and endurance if all you could bring to the bedroom was a three inch pee-pee no bigger around than a cocktail sausage. God what a mess she thought; I love Peter and my Peter can't give me any peter. Well, I'll just have to do my best to keep him happy and try to make sure that he never finds out just how big a slut his teeny tiny pee-pee has made me.

Her pussy was already tingling in anticipation as she walked off the elevator and headed for Jameson's office.

"Mary Jane, how good of you to come and my don't you look nice today."

"Cut the crap Jameson, we all know why I'm here and it isn't to be sociable. You gave Peter four assignments last week so I'm here to fulfill my part of the bargain. You want me on the desk, or bending over and leaning on it?"

"Neither, you big titted, redheaded slut. I want you on your knees sucking my cock."

"Are you going to be a gentleman and take it out for me, or make me risk breaking a nail trying to pull down your zipper?"

Jameson answered her by pulling his zipper down and taking out his cock. Not massive by any means, but it was still more than twice the size of Petey's and her mouth started watering as she leaned forward to take it into her mouth. She took his ball bag in her hands and caressed them as her tongue swirled around Jonah's cockhead and then with one slow, prolonged movement she swallowed his cock all the way to the base. Breathing through her nose she let her throat muscles work on Jonah's cock and then she slowly pulled back drawing a groan out of

Jameson as she did so. After that, it only took her sixty seconds of lip-clamped head bobbing to bring him off and she finished the job by sucking down every last drop of his fluid.

She stood up and turned to face Robby. "It's your turn now baby. Is that old Hershey stick ready for me?"

"Since an hour before you got here. I haven't thought of anything but your pussy all day."

"How sweet of you to say that. On the desk or over it?"

"Over it. Spread your legs wide, MJ, I want you from behind."

Mary Jane lifted her skirt, stepped out of her panties and then she leaned forward over the desk and spread her legs as wide as she could. Robby moved behind her and started sliding his hard cock into her hot snatch.

"Jesus, are you ever wet" Robby said.

And she was. She needed this fuck and had been looking forward to it all day so most of the juices were her own natural secretions. Most but not all. There had been the paperboy that morning when he had come to collect and she had paid him the way she always had – with a hot piece of ass – but Robby didn't need to know any of that. She did think it would be fun to wind Robby's watch so she said, "I know sweetie. Peter fucked me really good at lunch today and you are stroking into sloppy seconds. You don't mind, do you?"

Robby was buried to the hilt in MJ's hot pussy and he couldn't have cared less who was there before him; the only thing that counted was that he was there now. It could have been sloppy tenths and he still would have crawled over broken glass to sink his cock into her. There were times when Robby hated and despised J. Jonah Jameson, but never when he was fucking Mary Jane Parker. If it hadn't been for the way Jonah had played the red-haired beauty he would never have gotten the chance. Just once though, just once, he wished he could do her without a condom.

Mary Jane moaned as he bottomed out in her and he felt her pushing her ass back at him and he grabbed her hips and started fucking her long and hard which was what she seemed to like. Jameson came over and stuck his limp cock in the sexy redhead's face and she opened her mouth, took it in and started sucking him off. For the next hour, the two men took turns on Peter Parker's wife as she had several orgasms. She still wanted more cock and both Jonah and Robby wanted to give her more, but a look at the wall clock told MJ that she needed to head for home.

As she was leaving Jameson said, "Friday? Same time?"

"You know the deal Jameson. Four assignments gets you twice a week, once for every two assignments."

"One of these weeks Toots, I'm going to give him fourteen assignments and you will have to see me every day."

"Be careful Jameson. Let me at your cock for a week straight and I'll probably fuck you into a grave."

~~***~~

The limo stopped at a mid-town building that seemed to be under renovation and Kraven got out and went inside. Peter got out of the cab and paid off the cabbie and told him not to wait. When he decided to go home, he would web-swing it and savde on cab fare. He took a couple shots of Kraven walking into the building and talking to the workers. He noticed several large barred cages lined up against one wall and wondered what they might be used for. Nothing good if he knew Kraven and he was sure he did.

The Governor might have pardoned Kraven for his crimes against society, but Peter's Spidey Sense was never wrong and he felt the tingle running all the way down his spine. The man was up to no good and Spider-Man knew it. He glanced at his watch – time to get home to Mary Jane. Kraven had only been out of jail three days and that probably meant that he hadn't had time to set up much in the way of a plan so there was no sense sticking with him anymore that day. I'll pick up his trail tomorrow. Peter ducked behind a dumpster in an alley and when he came out from behind it he was ready to web-swing on home.

Three blocks is as far as he got before looking down to see a man snatch an old lady's purse and run with it. Spidey pointed his wrist at the fleeing man and a sound like 'Thwip' echoed among the tall buildings and the miscreant fell to the pavement with his feet wrapped in webbing. Spidey swung down and took the purse out of the thief's hands saying,

"Sorry Pal, but there isn't much I hate more than seeing a man carrying a purse. It just isn't manly."

The old lady came puffing up and Spidey handed her the purse and as he swung away from the scene, he heard the crook howling as the old lady beat on him with her umbrella.

~~***~~

"Hey MJ, I'm home."

"In the bedroom Petey."

Peter walked into the bedroom and found his wife lying nude on the bed, legs spread wide and finger fucking herself. "I've been waiting for you Tiger. I'm hot, wet and horny and I need your help here, baby. Come on Tiger, eat my hot pussy."

As Peter undressed, she smiled as she thought how glad she was that her husband was so gullible. He never doubted her when she told him that the wetness he sucked out of her was her natural juices. That was the only good thing that came out of his coming to their marriage bed a virgin. He had no experience, no way of knowing that her juiciness was not her natural secretions, but the cum deposits of her many lovers. Mary Jane was of mixed emotions on Peter's lack of experience. True, it gave her plenty of room to do the things she needed to do to gain sexual release, but it also allowed her to pull some pretty nasty tricks on him, like having him suck other men's cum out of her and that bothered her.

She loved Peter, she really did, but would she have married him had she known about his little wee-wee? She had to doubt it. She hadn't been a total slut going into her wedding night, but she had sampled a good half dozen or so cocks and she had already determined that size did indeed matter. Oh well, he didn't have much between his legs, but as a pussy eater he had no equal. As her husband buried his face in her cum loaded cunt she tried to remember just how many loads she had in her. The paperboy had cum in her twice that morning and Jameson had cum in her three – no, it was four times – and Robby had fucked her three times, but he didn't count because he was wearing a rubber, so she did have a pretty good puddle in her for Petey to lap up.

Poor Robby. He wanted to do her bareback so bad that he had offered her a thousand dollars. Damn. If she just had more faith and trust in her birth control pill and her diaphragm she'd take him up on it. Then again, if she didn't come up with a modeling assignment, a part in a TV show, play or movie pretty soon she just might have to chance it. Maybe her ass. She wondered if Robby would give her the grand if she let him cum in her butt. So far it was untapped territory. Well, Peter butt fucked her, but with his little cocktail weenie it was the same as being virgin ground. She would have to sound Robby out on that.

Peter was working his usual magic with his mouth and she felt her climax rushing in on her. She shook and a small contraction squeezed a blob of Jameson's cum out of her and into Peter's mouth and Mary Jane smiled as Peter swallowed it down.

For his part Peter loved hearing Mary Jane scream when he went down on her, but he wished that the spider bite that had changed his life hadn't made him such a sex maniac. He had to make love to Mary Jane once or twice a week to release his sexual frustrations and it had an effect on the quality of their love making. He remembered how tight her pussy had been on their wedding night and he wished he could feel it again, but Mary Jane had pointed out that the more sex they had the looser she would be.

"You might want me to tighten up Tiger, but I don't think I can ever leave you alone long enough for that to happen. I need my sex baby, so you better get used to making love to me at least once a week."

Peter wondered if maybe there might be a pill that worked just the opposite of Viagra. If he could just stop being a sex fiend and needing sex once or twice a week and back off to maybe just twice a month Mary Jane would have time to tighten back up.

Mary Jane was just coming off of her eighth or ninth orgasm of the day and she felt exhausted.

"I'm beat from pounding the pavement all day looking for work Tiger. If you are going to make love to me better hurry up. That super orgasm you just gave me took a lot out of me and I don't want to fall asleep on you."

Peter mounted her and as was usually the case she didn't even know he was in her, but he was humping so she made the requisite noises and moans and moved her body around in simulated passion while she thought about which of her many lovers she would see the next day.

Chapter 2

Peter was out the door at the crack of dawn armed with his cameras. He hoped to get some good shots of Kraven to go with the ones he had taken the previous day. He headed for the building where he had left Kraven the night before. He intended to find out what Kraven's interest in the place was.

There were two men sitting at a table just inside the door, sipping coffee and going over blueprints. He identified himself as a reporter/photographer for the Daily Bugle, gave them a song and dance about how the paper was going to do a series on new construction and renovations in the downtown and then asked them what the place they were working on was going to be.

"It is going to be some kind of weird exotic restaurant with wild animals in cages scattered around the room."

Peter looked at the man in disbelief, "You can't be serious."

"Oh but I am. Look right here on the print," and he pointed to a spot.

Peter looked and sure enough it showed where the crocodile cage was to be placed. He noticed cage locations for other animals – lions and tigers and bears – "Oh my," he said, "has anybody thought about the natural stink of these animals and what they will do to the patron's appetite? Imagine sitting at a table next to the lion cage just getting ready to dig into a steak when the lion decides to take a dump."

"Hey mac, not my problem. I just get paid to do the construction."

"Thanks for the information," Peter said as he got ready to leave.

"Hey mac, don't you want my picture? You know, for the story?"

"Yeah, sure," Peter said and he wasted an exposure taking the guys picture.

The building maintenance man was lying on his back looking up at the sink that Mary Jane had said was leaking. He wasn't surprised when he felt his zipper being pulled down. Three or four times a week Mary Jane called him to come to her apartment and work on something although it was usually Mary Jane who did all the work. Like now, for instance. Her left hand was on the countertop bracing herself as she squatted over him and used her right hand to guide his erection into her cunt.

He just laid there and enjoyed it as she worked herself up and down on his shaft. Sweet Jesus was she good and he hoped that she never moved out of the building. The phone rang and Mary Jane picked the cordless up off of the counter and answered it.

"Hello?"

"Oh, hi honey."

"Nothing much, just getting my morning exercise. I'm doing squats right now. Have to keep my body nice and tight and attractive for you."

The pure sluttishness of talking to her husband while fucking Stan fired Mary Jane up and she began moving faster up and down the maintenance man's pole.

"Nothing baby, I always breathe hard when I exercise. I'm in the middle of a really hard work out right now."

"Maybe."

"I'll try, but I can't promise. If I get a call for an interview I won't be able to, but if no one calls I'll see you there."

"Not really baby, right now I'm really feeling the burn."

"Bye sweetie, I love you too."

"My husband wants me to have lunch with him Stan. Help me work up an appetite," she said as she slammed down on his hard cock.

~~***~~

Mary Jane was feeling good. And she was proud of herself. It had taken her less than two minutes to suck Stan's cock hard again for their second fuck of the morning. The second time was on her bed and with Stan on top and she wondered if he would have bruises on the backs of his legs where her heels had drummed against them. It only took her three minutes to get him up for the third romp. That one was doggie style. She loved taking a long, hard cock from the rear and she enjoyed the hell out of Stan. He was young, he was energetic and he had a large cock and she liked those qualities in a man.

He left and she started to get ready to make the rounds of the modeling agencies. She debated between douching or leaving Stan in her so Petey could suck him out. She did get a lot of wicked pleasure out of Petey's sucking her lover's leavings out of her before tickling her with his little stub, but she did have an agency she wanted to visit and if they had a casting couch she didn't want to jeopardize her chances by giving some one sloppy seconds.

She got up and headed for the bathroom just as the phone rang.

"Hello?"

"Ms. Parker?"

"This is she."

"Ms. Parker, I am Adam Zimmer and I am the talent coordinator for Safari Productions. My principal would like to talk with you about a part in a movie he is planning. Would you be free for lunch today?"

"Well, I did have some plans, but nothing that I can't reschedule."

"Good. Adolpho's at one?"

"Yes, I can be there."

"Excellent. Just give the hostess your name, she will know to expect you."

"Oh my God," Mary Jane thought as she hung up the phone, "a part in a movie. I wonder if it is a speaking part or just a walk on. Hell, I don't care. It is exposure and it could lead to something else. Oh oh, no lunch with Peter today. Petey, what to do about Petey. Let's see, business lunch so it should last an hour to an hour and a half, no casting couches in restaurants so even if I do have to put out to get the part it won't be today. No need to douche then so I can leave Stan inside me for Petey tonight."

She looked at her watch and saw that she needed to hurry if she was to look her best for the meeting.

"Is she coming?" Kraven asked.

"She said she would be there."

"How is work at the warehouse coming?"

"The sets are all made and painted. The camera equipment arrived this morning and the crew and supporting cast are already here and ready to go. All we need is our star."

"If things go right I'll have her this afternoon."

"You sure about this? Granted that her husband is only freelance, but he does have ties to the local media."

"It won't matter. If she is the fame hungry twit we think she is she will control him until we have what we want. After that? Who cares what he thinks or who he has ties to. But then again, maybe it would serve us better if she were a widow. Yes, I think that is the way to go. See to it."

"Yes sir."

~~***~~

Peter stood at the front gate of the prison and looked up at the high walls. It was an austere and imposing structure and one well suited for housing society's miscreants. Since he had called ahead, the guards were expecting him and a half-hour later he was sitting in the warden's office.

"I know what you told me on the phone Mr. Parker, but just what is your interest in this case?"

"It's like I told you Warden Jones, I'm doing a piece on rehabilitation and I thought the situation involving Kraven The Hunter would be the perfect backdrop for the story. How does a criminal – a menace to society – come into a place like this and have his life turned around in just a few short years? How do you turn him into a man that the Governor himself sees fit to pardon and return to society."

Peter listened to the psycho-babble of the warden without learning what he had hoped to learn. He had hoped to learn something that would let him get ahead of Kraven on whatever Kraven was planning. Peter wanted to be ahead of the curve for a change, not reacting to what the criminal did as was usually the case. Peter left the prison with no more idea of what Kraven was up to than he'd had when he got up this morning.

~~***~~

Mary Jane recognized him as she approached the table. Kraven The Hunter. He was a big man and he had an aura of power around him. She took in the wide shoulders and big biceps and she felt a tingle in her loins. She wondered if he had a cock that matched the rest of him as far as size went. She almost came in her panties as she wondered what it would be like to fuck a man that her husband had sent to prison. She smiled as she thought that if she got the part she might just find out. It would be a kick to take home a load of cum from one of Petey's archenemies and have Petey suck it all out of her.

Kraven rose as she approached the table. "Ms. Parker, so nice of you to come on such short notice."

"The pleasure is all mine. I've heard so much about you."

"Not all of it good I'll wager."

"Does it have to be? All women like to see a touch of 'bad boy' in a man."

"Oh my dear Ms. Parker, I like you all ready. Well, I suppose Adam told you what this meeting is all about?"

"He did mention a part in a movie."

"A part in a movie? Oh no Ms. Parker, not just a part."

"Please call me Mary Jane."

"I want you for my leading lady, Mary Jane."

Mary Jane had just kicked off a high heel and was getting ready to run her foot up Kraven's leg suddenly pulled it back. She had been prepared to fuck Kraven's brains out to get the part, but from the way he was talking he had already decided to give her much more than just a small part. No sense in letting him think she was an easy slut even though she was. Once she was sure of what was going on she would fuck him to death as a way of saying thank you.

It did leave her with one small problem though. Her interlude with Stan this morning had been nice, but she had expected to get another taste sometime during the day. Now she wished she and Stan had gone another time or three.

Kraven said, "I propose that we go to my office to talk about what I have in mind and to discuss contracts."

Mary Jane smiled at him and said, "sounds like a plan."

~~***~~

Peter's jaw almost hit the sidewalk in disbelief as he saw Mary Jane come out of Adolpho's on the arm of Kraven. It explained why she hadn't answered the phone when he'd called her to tell her where to meet him for lunch, but what was she doing with Kraven? A limousine pulled up and Kraven helped Mary Jane get in and then he followed her and the limo pulled away from the curb. Peter looked around for a cab, but there wasn't a blob of yellow anywhere on the street. A quick look showed him a dark hallway. He didn't like to web swing during the day, but he had to know where Kraven was going with Mary Jane.

As the limousine moved down the Avenue of the America's, Mary Jane's thoughts were on "The Red Carpet" and she was already hearing the commentary of Joan Rivers and her daughter Mellisa. She smiled inwardly as she saw herself accepting Oscars, Emmys, Golden

Globes and the like and then she noticed people looking up and pointing and she asked Kraven if he knew what was going on.

Kraven pushed a button and the sunroof opened up and she and Kraven looked up and saw Spider-Man swing along and looking down at them.

"I knew it would happen sooner or later."

"Knew what would happen?"

"That the web-head would start harassing me."

"I'm sure you're mistaken."

"I don't think so. I've only been in town three days and there he is hovering over me."

"But this is his territory. People see him every day swinging over these streets."

"I don't mean to sound rude Mary Jane, but unlike you, I know him and I know what the wall crawler is doing. He was responsible for putting me in prison and my being out is like a personal affront to him. He will be doing his best to see me sent back."

A retort was on the tip of her tongue, but at the last second she beat down the loyalty to her husband that was going to make her speak. It wouldn't change Kraven's mind, but it could cost her her chance to be a star.

~~***~~

Peter stayed with the limo until it pulled up in front of the Hilton. Kraven got out of the car and looked up at him and then gave him the one-fingered salute. Then Kraven helped Mary Jane out of the limo and the two of them disappeared into the hotel. Peter was shut down. He could web-swing and wall-crawl and get away with it, but he couldn't get away with looking in hotel windows, at least not during the day. He had no way of finding out what was going on between Mary Jane and Kraven inside the Hilton. Since he had seen them coming out of Adolpho's it didn't seem likely that they were going to be in the restaurant. That left only one possibility – Kraven was taking Mary Jane to his room!

As Kraven led Mary Jane into the elevator she asked, "Where are we going?"

"To my office."

"But this is a hotel."

"I have a suite of rooms, two of which are set up as offices. My staff uses one and I use the other."

This could be dangerous Mary Jane thought. I know I said I would hold off until later to spread for the man, but can I hold off if I'm in a hotel room with him? Do I want to? I know Petey saw us come in and he is probably outside right now furious that he can't know what Kraven is up to. Wouldn't it be deliciously wicked to fuck Kraven with Petey outside watching the building and then go home to him full of Kraven's juices? She glanced over at Kraven. From the bulge in his trousers it would seem that he wanted to put some pipe to her.

Kraven noticed the slut eyeing his package. He hadn't expected that he would be able to put her on her back so soon, but fucking her now or fucking her later didn't matter all that much as far as his plans for her went. She was a hot looking piece so maybe the sooner he started the more he could enjoy her before he had to end it. He would see how it went. Maybe he was misreading her; after all, she was a married woman.

The first thing that Mary Jane saw when they entered Kraven's suite was the king size bed. Kraven saw her notice the bed and he also noticed that she made no protest and that she didn't run screaming from the room. Kraven took her by the arm and led her through the connecting door that led into a fully furnished office. Was that a look of disappointment he saw in her eyes?

There was another connecting door in the opposite wall and it was open and she saw a man working at a desk. Kraven offered Mary Jane a seat in front of his desk and he left the door behind him open and Mary Jane wondered if it was deliberate. From where she was sitting, she had a clear view of Kraven's bed. Could he be that devious? Even as she asked herself that question she knew that the answer was yes. She knew she was going to fuck Kraven sooner or later and Kraven knew he was going to fuck her. All that was needed was for the two of them to communicate and Mary Jane knew that she could find a way to give him an opening. She just hadn't decided if she was going to give him the opening today.

"Well, let's get down to business, shall we? I have already decided that I want you for my lead, but you haven't yet decided that you want to be my star. You know nothing of the project and you may take one look at the script and then say 'Sorry, not for me.' We can save each other a lot of time with one question. How do you feel about partial nudity?"

"I can't honestly answer that question because I don't know your definition of 'partial.' Does it mean topless? Or maybe unclothed, but with strategically placed leaves and twigs? I need more information."

"There is one scene in the movie where you will be bathing in a river. It is basically a nude scene, but from the back only. We can put pasties or a partial body stocking on your front, but your backside would be completely uncovered. Could you do that?"

"If it was tastefully done, yes I could do that."

"Okay then, let's move on. Toward the middle of the picture there will be several scenes where your costume wouldn't be much more than a two piece bathing suit."

"No problem there. In my modeling career I have done hundreds of lingerie ads, a lot of them just bra and panties."

"This would not be the same. When you model it is static. You know, 'Turn a little left, look up, hold it' the picture is taken and you move on to the next pose. In moving pictures, it is different. You will be running around, bras will be slipping, your boobs will be swinging – you will be moving. What I'm asking is can you run around half naked in front of fifteen or twenty cast and crew members?"

"I don't see why not."

"Okay, we will check that out later. Here's what we are doing. You know of my wildlife and environmental work that got me my pardon?"

"Yes, it was in the papers."

"I have found a wealthy backer and I'm going to parlay my love for wild animals into a feature film. I'm going to jump on the 'remake' wagon and remake 'Tarzan' from a current perspective. Same as the original premise – boy raised by apes – and then an expedition is formed to search out the fabled Ape Man. The expedition wanders into an area they were told to stay clear of and the end up between the two warring factions in the civil war that was taking place in the Congo. You are the only survivor and you only survive because Tarzan saves you."

"Then he tries to get you back to civilization before you are killed by hunter/killer teams from the two factions so you cannot tell the world press about the massacre of the expedition. The subplot is that both sides in the civil war are allowing poachers, for a fee, to hunt down and kill the wild animals that are so much a part of the African continent. The purpose of the film, in addition to its entertainment value is to alert the world to the slaughter of the animals in Africa."

"Who are you looking at for the role of Tarzan?"

"Brad Pitt has shown an interest and we are in negotiations."

"Brad Pitt?"

"Yes."

"Damn it to hell."

"What?"

"He and Jennifer Aniston have split and he's back on the market. He'll be my co-star, but I'm married. Ain't that just my luck?"

"I take it you want the part?"

"Yes I do."

"Well, I'm a little embarrassed by this, but I need to satisfy myself on a point."

"What's that?"

"Would you please strip down to your underwear?"

"What?"

"I want to see if you can run around scantily clad in front of an audience made up of crew and cast members. If you can't do it in front of us, I doubt that you could do it front of a crew."

"Us?"

"Yes, us. I'll call Adam and his associate in here. If you can do it you have the lead."

"Oh I can do it all right; if it is on the up and up."

"I'm hurt Mary Jane. Tsk, tsk, to think that you don't trust me."

He opened a briefcase and took out a sheaf of paper, signed the last page and handed it to her.

"It is your contract and I've already signed it. All you have to do is what I asked for, sign the contract and give it back to me. Although, if you are as smart as I think you are, I hope you will read it first."

Mary Jane took the contract, glanced at it and then put it in her purse. She stood up, "Get the audience in here."

Kraven picked up the phone and pushed a button. "Andy, get Joe and come into my office. Leave Mark to answer the phones and talk to any walk-ins."

A minute later two men walked into the office. One was a short, balding man and the other was a tall well-built black man. By then Mary Jane was out of her blouse and was just stepping out of her skirt. She did a couple of slow turns in front of the men and then she took off her bra and thong and tossed them into the middle of Kraven's desk.

"What do you think boys," she asked as she tweaked her nipples, "is this a good rack?" She tweaked her nipples with her fingers and said, "maybe you would like to suck on them? Maybe tit fuck me?"

She gave the three men a dazzling smile and the she strutted into the bedroom and spread herself out on the king size bed and waited to see what the three men would do.

Peter was driving himself crazy wondering what his wife was doing with Kraven. Seeing her come out of Adolpho's on Kraven's arm was a shock to his system, but nothing compared to the feelings he was having after seeing her go into a mid-town hotel with Kraven. How did she meet him? Why was she with him at all, let alone be in a hotel with him. She knew that he had been responsible for sending Kraven to prison and at the time she had even congratulated him on doing it. And now she was with him?

He went into the hotel and checked out the restaurant, the bar, and even the meeting rooms, but he didn't find either his wife or Kraven. He really didn't want to do it, but it was the only way he could think of to find out what was going on. He went to the front desk and showed his press-pass to the desk clerk.

"I'm Peter Parker and I'm here to interview Kraven The Hunter for an article I'm doing for the Daily Bugle."

"Peter Parker? Aren't you the one who gets all those great photos of Spider-Man?"

"You really think they are great?"

"I sure do, and something else; I don't care what that asshole J. Jonah Jameson says, I think Spider-Man is a hero. Just the other day he stopped a thief who snatched my grandmother's purse."

"I'm sure Spidey would be happy to hear that."

She punched some keys and looked at her computer screen. "Mr. Kraven has a suite of rooms on the ninth floor. He is using room 914 as an office."

Peter thanked her and headed for the elevators.

~~***~~

Kraven approached the naked red-haired beauty spread out for him on his bed. As he undid his belt he said, "why Mrs. Parker, what would your husband say?"

"Peter and I adhere to a modified Clinton policy."

"Modified Clinton policy? I don't believe that I've ever heard of that."

"Clinton's policy on gays in the military was 'Don't ask, don't tell.' I've modified that policy to fit situations like this. Peter is too dumb to ask, and I'm too smart to tell."

"Why are you doing this? You already have the part so there is no need to play the casting couch game."

"Oh, but I do have to do it. I have to prove to you that I can be comfortable performing in front of a crew. It should be obvious by the time I get done with the four of you that I can handle being naked on the set."

"Four of us? There are only three. Joe, Andy and me."

"You mean one of you won't go and relieve Mark so he can share in the wealth?"

"Whatever you want Mary Jane, whatever your little heart desires," and Kraven let his trousers and boxers fall to the floor.

"Oooh" cried Mary Jane, "I do hope that is all you and not some movie special effects."

"If you think this is big, wait until you see Joe's."

"I'm glad you brought that up. Joe honey, my pussy is an equal opportunity receptacle, but if you want to fuck me you need to use a rubber. White babies I can blame on my husband, but even as dumb as my Peter is when it comes to sexual matters, there just isn't any way I'd be able to convince him that he fathered a black one. If cumming in my soft, white body is something you just have to do, you can do it in my mouth. I'll suck you off baby, and then I'll swallow every drop. That said, come on Kravey baby, bring me that big, beautiful log."

As the elevator headed up toward the ninth floor Peter began to worry about what he would say to MJ if he found her. He couldn't let her know that he was following her. And he knew what she would say if he said he was worried about her because she was with Kraven. She would get all pissed off at him.

"Honestly Peter, I'm a big girl now and I can take care of myself."

But she couldn't. There wasn't any way that MJ could handle Kraven's brute strength.

Mary Jane could have argued that point with him because at the exact instant Peter had had that thought she was handling Kraven's brute strength very well. In fact, she had the big man breathing hard and working up a sweat as he pounded his large cock into her. Mary Jane had already had one orgasm and was pretty close to having her second when she felt something hot touch her cheek. She opened her eyes and saw Joe's cock inches from her mouth.

"Give it to me baby, I love chocolate" and she opened her mouth to accept the black man's cock as he scooted forward on his knees.

Chapter 3

Peter checked out the room numbers as he walked down the hall. When he got to room 914 he wondered if the desk clerk had gotten it right. He knew that he was reasonably close to the right place because his Spider Sense was tingling enough to tell him that Kraven was close by and doing something that he shouldn't be. But room 914 didn't look like an office; it looked like the door to any other hotel room. He tried the door and was surprised when it opened under his hand.

He walked into a room that was obviously a hotel room converted to an office. It was the same as any other hotel room Peter had been in except where the bed should be there was a desk and a small table with four chairs. A young man was sitting behind the desk and he looked up as Peter came into the room.

"Yes sir? Can I help you?"

"I hope so. I'm Peter Parker and I'm with the Daily Bugle. I was wondering if Mr. Kraven could spare a minute or two of his time. We want to do a story on him."

"I'm not sure he can see you right now. He and our talent coordinator are busy plugging up a few holes that came up in relation to a movie Mr. Kraven is making. Why don't you take a seat and I'll go see if he can break free."

Peter took a seat on one of the chairs at the table and the young man got up and left the room.

~~***~~

Mary Jane had her lips locked around Joe's fat, black cock and her head was rocking back and forth on it. Kraven had pulled her legs up onto his shoulders and he was ramming her pussy with deep hard strokes. She was on her third or fourth orgasm – they were coming so close it was hard to tell – when Kraven hissed, "here it comes Mrs. Parker, here it comes," and he erupted into her and splashed her insides with his manly essence.

He saw Andy standing next to the bed, stroking himself and patiently waiting so he pulled himself out of the lusty red-haired slut and said, "your turn Andy."

There was a knock at the door and then it opened just enough for Mark to stick his head in and say, "hope I'm not interrupting anything, but we have a rather droll situation here. It seems that the lady's husband has come to call and he begs an audience with you."

"What?"

"I have Mr. Parker in the office. He would like a few minutes of your time. Something about an article that he is working on for the Daily Bugle."

"Her husband huh? By all means tell him that I'll be there to see him in a minute."

Kraven smiled as he took his right hand and stroked his cock to coat it with Mary Jane's juices. As he quickly dressed he watched the action on the bed and wondered if Mary Jane had heard Mark. Joe was lying on his back on the bed and Mary Jane was on her hands and knees as Andy fucked her from behind while she slobbered all over Joe's massive black cock. Kraven wondered if there was some way he could stall Parker long enough to get back to the room and fuck Parker's wife one more time while her husband was less than fifty feet away.

Mary Jane had indeed heard what Mark had said and her reaction surprised her. Andy's cock wasn't all that big compared to Joe's and Kraven's and it wasn't pushing her buttons like Kraven's had. She was nowhere near an orgasm, that is she wasn't until she heard Mark say that

Peter was here and just down the hall. Suddenly, the thought of how deliciously wicked and depraved it was to be fucking three men while Petey was so close by triggered a very large orgasm in her. Her cunt spasmed and to Andy it felt like she had a hand in her pussy jacking him off. It was too much for him and he blew his load into her steaming cunt. As he pulled out of her boiling cauldron, Mary Jane cried out, "no, not yet, stay in, leave it in."

Andy looked at his boss and shrugged and Kraven laughed.

"Saddle up Mark. The slut needs meat in her box and she won't let Joe in because he doesn't have a condom so it looks like you just volunteered. You guys keep her hot and going till I get back from talking to the cuckold."

~~***~~

Peter stood up when Kraven walked into the room with his right hand stuck out in greeting. Peter took the hand and shook it and was surprised at the dampness of the big man's palm. Must have just washed his hands.

"Mr. Parker, what can I do for you?"

"Parker, Parker, for some reason that name rings a bell. Oh yes, now I remember. You took the pictures of me and Spider-Man that appeared on the front page of the Bugle."

"Guilty. I just happened to be in the right place at the right time; or from your perspective, the right place at the wrong time."

"It wasn't one of my finer moments, but with hindsight I do have to say that it was one of the best things to happen to me."

"Say what?"

"That surprises you, does it? The truth of the matter is that in sending me to prison, Spider-Man changed my life. Prison had a positive influence on my life" and the big man laughed. "I'm positive that I don't want to go back. So positive that I decided to turn my life around. I took all the energy and intellect that I used to devote to my nefarious activities and channeled them toward good works. It was my work on environmental issues that got me pardoned. That came as a surprise to me and it reinforced my resolve to do good for my fellowmen and my planet."

What a load of bullshit Peter thought. If he were on the level, my Spider Sense would be silent instead of making me want to web him and tie him down before he can commit a crime. But how do I steer this conversation to why he was with MJ. And where is she? She still must be here some place because I would have seen her if she left. Then again, maybe I wouldn't have. The desk clerk said this was a suite of rooms. Maybe she went out one of the other doors while I was sitting here waiting for Kraven. But that brings me right back to the question, "what is my wife doing in a hotel room with Kraven?" His thoughts were interrupted by Kraven.

"So, what is it I can do for you Mr. Parker."

"I'm sure that you must know that your release from prison has stirred the public interest. J. Jonah Jameson, the owner and publisher of the Daily Bugle says you are news and he wants pictures of you. I'm a freelance photographer, but I'm trying to move up in the world. I want to be a photojournalist. I can follow you around and take candid shots, but that won't get me where I want to go. What I would really like to do is write a story to go along with the photos. To that end, I would like to ask you just what your plans are, how you hope to help the environment now that you are a free man and other things along those lines."

"I have several irons in the fire right now. My major concern is the disastrous poaching that is going on in Africa. Whole species are in danger of becoming extinct. I'm not silly enough to think that I can go over there and single handedly put a stop to it; the best I can do is try to make the public aware of what is happening. If I can stir up the public enough perhaps they will go to their representatives and senators. Get to enough of them and the government can put pressure on the African despots to get them to do what must be done to stop the poachers."

"How can you do that?"

"You have to convince people that the animals are worth saving. To do that I have to show them how magnificent the animals are. One thing I am going to do is open a theme based restaurant where I will have wild animals on display. Not the tame and mangy looking animals you see in the zoo, but animals from the wild just off the boat from Africa.

"The other thing I'm doing is making a full length feature film. It is a remake of Tarzan, but set in modern times and it will show him battling the poachers and trying to save the animals. In fact, I have started casting already. I just signed the female lead today. By an odd coincidence her name is Parker too. Could she be related to you?"

"What is her full name?"

"Mary Jane Parker."

"As a matter of fact we are related; she is my wife."

"All I can say to that is you lucky devil you. Let me get you a brochure that lays out the plans for Kraven The Hunter, Limited. We are forming a foundation for the preservation of wildlife and the brochure spells out our aims. Don't go away, I'll be right back."

Kraven returned to the bedroom to find Mary Jane sucking Andy's cock while Joe was long dicking her from the rear.

"She changed her mind about Joe needing a raincoat?"

"No," Mark said, "I had one in my wallet that I let him have."

"Are you close Joe? I want to fuck her one more time while her husband is still here."

"Almost boss, just a little more and I'll shoot."

"Mark, go and keep the twit company. Show him our plans for the restaurant, but keep him there while I fuck his wife."

"Okay boss. Do I get seconds?"

"You can fuck the slut as much as you want for as long as she can stay with us."

On the bed Joe gave out a combination moan and groan as he came in the slut wife and then he pulled out. Mary Jane rolled over onto her back and spread her legs wide while pulling her knees back to her chest. "Come on Kravey baby, fuck me and make me scream while my husband is just down the hall."

Kraven looked down on the insatiable slut and thought that he might just have to change his plans for her. He just might want to keep her around for a while.

Chapter 4

While Peter waited for Kraven to return with the brochure of the Kraven The Hunter Wild Life Foundation, he wondered if maybe he wasn't over-reacting. Kraven's aims were good ones and the man did sound sincere. If it wasn't for the Spider Sense he could have bought into what Kraven had said. On the one hand, his Spider Sense had never been wrong, but that wasn't to say that there couldn't be a first time. What if the man was sincere and prison had turned him around? What if the Spider Sense was just some residual from their last encounter? Should he give the man the benefit of the doubt? He really didn't have an answer to that question.

Had Peter the x-ray vision of Superman and could he have seen through the two walls that currently separated him from Kraven, he would have had no problem answering that question. Kraven had the legs of Peter's wife up on his shoulders and he was ramming his cock into her accommodating cunt. Andy and Joe were kneeling on the bed on either side of her head and Mary Jane was alternating between their cocks. MJ felt Andy's cock start to throb and she locked her lips around it and reached a hand up to caress his balls and when he spurted it hit the back of her throat and she swallowed it down. She held him in her mouth until he was soft and then she let his dick fall from her lips and turned her head to take on Joe's cock.

As she opened her mouth to take it, she made a mental note to start carrying condoms in her purse. Cocks as big as Joe's belonged in her pussy. At least she had gotten to have that huge log slide into her one time thanks to the rubber that Mark had in his wallet. She glanced at her watch and saw that it was only two-thirty. Kraven noticed and said, "in a hurry to leave Mrs. Parker?"

"Not at all stud. I just wanted to see how much more time I have to enjoy this."

"And just how much time do we have Mrs. Parker?"

"I have to be home by six. Think you and your crew can keep up with me for another two and a half hours?"

"I wouldn't be the least bit surprised, Mrs. Parker."

"Call me Mary Jane."

"Oh no, you are Mrs. Parker as long as Mr. Parker is in the next room. There is just something so superbly erotic in fucking a married woman while her husband is so close and unaware."

At the reminder that Peter was within hollering distance Mary Jane's body trembled as she had another orgasm.

"Why Mrs. Parker. I do believe that you are turned on by the idea."

"Shut up and fuck me, Kravey baby, fuck me, fuck me hard."

~~***~~

Mark entered the room and saw Peter Parker sitting there patiently and he smiled to himself as he thought about what a hot piece of ass Parker's wife was. He hoped he would get a couple of more chances at her hot box before the afternoon was over. Like Kraven and Mary Jane herself, he thought of how erotic it had been to be fucking Parker's wife while Parker was sitting in the outer office blissfully unaware of what his wife was doing just two rooms – less than fifty feet – away from where he was sitting.

"Mr. Kraven offers his apologies Mr. Parker. He received an urgent phone call and he had to take it. He will be back shortly. While you are waiting can I get you something? Coffee or perhaps a soft drink?"

"No, thank you. Do you have any idea how long Mr. Kraven's call will take?"

Mark looked at his watch, "He should be finishing any time now."

~~***~~

Two doors over Kraven grunted, "here it comes you fucking married slut. I'm cumming Mrs. Parker, I'm cummimg."

"Give it to me Kravey, fill Mrs. Parker's pussy with your juice. Shoot your jizz deep into Peter's pussy."

~~***~~

Mark smiled at Peter; "while we are waiting can I show the plans for our theme based restaurant?"

Peter had already seen the plans when he had visited the construction site earlier in the day, but he needed Kraven and his crew to think that he was really working on a story so he said, "yes thank you, I'd like that."

Mark opened a file cabinet and took out a rolled up set of blueprints and spread them out across the desk. He was pointing out the location of the monkey cages when Kraven came back into the room. The familiar tingle ran up and down Peter's spine again. If the Spider Sense was accurate Kraven had either just been up to no good or was in the process of doing something no good.

"Damn!" thought Petey, "just once I'd like to be ahead of the bad guy and not just have to react to what he's done."

"Sorry about the wait," Kraven said, "but that call was from the CEO of a rather large corporation who wanted to make a sizeable donation to the Wild Life Fund. Speaking of which, here is the brochure on the fund that I said I would get for you."

Peter took the folder and as he opened it and started to read it Kraven said, "is there anything else I can do for you? If not I have some serious business to get back to. I have something that I really want to stay on top of."

"Just one more thing. Could I get a picture of you sitting behind your desk?"

"Certainly, but only if you give me a minute to straighten it up. Mark, go over the information in the folder with Mr. Parker while I sanitize my desk."

Kraven hurried to the bedroom and told Andy and Joe to get off of the redheaded slut and then he took her by the hand and pulled her naked body along behind him into his office.

"I need you to get under my desk."

"What for?"

"No time to talk, but if you got a kick out of fucking us with your husband in the outer office, you'll love this."

Mary Jane crawled under Kraven's desk as he walked away. A minute later he returned and she almost had an orgasm when she realized what Kraven was up to. She heard him say, "I have no idea why the Bugle would like a picture of me behind my desk, but any publicity at all will help my foundation."

Kraven sat down at his desk and scooted the chair forward and Mary Jane almost broke a nail in her haste to get his fly open and his cock in her mouth. She just had to have that hunk of meat in her mouth when Petey took Kraven's picture.

Peter's Spider Sense was screaming and his hands were shaking so bad that he was having trouble focusing the camera. Damn it, what was the man up to?

Mary Jane's tongue was laving the head of Kraven's cock when she heard the 'click' of the shutter as Petey took the picture. She swallowed as much of Kraven's cock as she could and then slowly bobbed her head up and down on it as much as the desk would allow while she waited for Peter to take the backup shot. God but did she feel so wicked. She just wished that Kraven could be ejaculating down her throat just as the camera clicked, but she had already taken so much cum out of him that she knew he was a long way from being able to give her another load. Still the experience would help her get off for a long time to come.

~~***~~

Peter took the elevator up to the top floor and then made his way up to the roof. Assuming his Spider-Man identity he sat on the roof ledge and looked out over the city. He was in trouble and he knew it. Regardless of what Kraven said, he was a career criminal. He might have changed in prison, but it was only a change in the way he did things – "I got caught doing it that way so let's make a change and do it some other way."

The man was up to something and Spidey knew it, and that is where the trouble was going to come from. Kraven had just signed Mary Jane for a movie. Peter knew how MJ viewed her career. Mary Jane would do anything short of going to bed with whomever it was who would offer her a chance to be a star. If he tried to warn her about Kraven she would go ballistic on him. She would accuse him of being jealous of her fame; tell him that he couldn't stand to see her become famous while he had to hide from his own fame as Spider-Man.

Peter shook his head. Mary Jane was very photogenic and did okay as a model, but she had zero talent as an actress. The only way she could achieve any fame in the movie business was if she totally flipped out and started making porno movies. God knows she had the talent for that. Thank God he was the only one who would ever know that.

~~***~~

He stood up and shot a strand of webbing across to the next building and started to web swing around town. He hadn't been five minutes in the air when something on the ground caught his eye. He swung down to take a closer look. The two teenagers who were stealing the hubcaps off of the Cadillac didn't hear him as he hit the ground softly behind them.

"Come on guys, you aren't going to make me waste webbing over a hub cap or two, are you?"

The two boys jerked around, saw Spider-Man and took off running. Spidey watched them go, "must have been something I said," and then he put the loose hubcaps back on the car.

~~***~~

Mary Jane looked at the four men. "No one? Not one of you can help a poor girl out? Come on guys, I'm just one weak little girl here; surely one of you big strong men can get it up one more time. No? You going to make me go home horny?"

Kraven, Andy, Joe and Mark all looked at each other and shrugged, half ashamed at not being able to help Mary Jane out. She looked at her watch, "oh well, I guess it is time for me to be going anyway. Probably just as well we don't go again."

She began to dress and then she straightened up and asked Kraven, "what is my schedule going to be Kravey? When do we go into rehearsals and when do I see the script?"

"Be here tomorrow at nine and we will start going over the schedule."

"All of you going to be here?"

"Probably."

"Take your vitamins boys. You don't want to get in the habit of letting a girl down."

Mark said, "any way we can get doofus to be here tomorrow? I got a hell of a charge doing you while he was waiting down the hall."

"What did you call him?" Mary Jane coldly asked him.

"Doofus. I mean what else could he be if you have to get your meat away from home."

"My husband's name is Peter, not doofus. If you enjoyed what you got today you will remember that. I will not have you clowns making disparaging remarks about the man I love. You got that?"

Kraven smiled, but Joe, Andy and Mark all looked away from Mary Jane and mumbled that yes, they understood her.

"As for getting, as you so crudely put it, my meat away from home, consider this. I'm standing here wanting a cock and I can't get one because I wore the four of you out. My husband is only one man; if the four of you can't stay with me why would you think that one of him could?"

She glared at all four men in turn and then she started gathering her clothes.

~~***~~

As Peter was swinging off the roof Mary Jane was in the elevator heading down to the lobby. She glanced at her watch. Normally, she wouldn't be in any hurry to get home, but today she figured it would be a very good idea to beat Peter home so she could clean up a bit. God, but she couldn't believe how big a slut she had been. She knew she was a slut – poor Peter had seen to that – but before that day she had never done more than one man at a time. She had had more than one at a sitting, like Jameson and Robby, but she only had fucked them one at a time, not the two of them together at the same time. Today she had spent the whole afternoon with two cocks in her at the same time. Mark had wanted to make it three – he wanted her ass bad – but she wouldn't give her butt hole up. So far Petey was the only one who had gone there and she had always felt she needed to keep something just for him.

It had been great; it had been marvelous, stupendous even, and she couldn't wait to do it again. But she did need to beat Petey home. She had so much sperm in her that she sloshed when she walked. If she didn't get some of it out of her before she sat on his face she might drown him and the one thing she knew for sure was that she was going to sit on his face. No way was she going to pass up the chance of getting Peter to slurp up a little of the cum of the man he had put into prison. She wondered if Lois Lane ever considered letting Lex Luther fuck her so she could sit on Superman's face and feed him some of his archenemy's cum.

"Oh, and while I'm at it I'd better get some condoms to carry in my purse. I don't want to have to pass up any more cocks like Joe's just because the guy didn't come prepared."

~~***~~

After Mary Jane had gone, Kraven had turned to Andy, "have the arrangements for Mr. Parker's demise been made?"

"Yes sir. In fact, it was supposed to happen this afternoon. I contacted our man and told him Parker was here so he could follow Parker when he left, but then I called it off."

"Why would you do that?"

"I didn't want to risk the police getting to his body with the last pictures in his camera being of you."

"Good thinking Andy. But we need to make it happen soon. I believe I'm going to accelerate the timetable where Mrs. Parker is concerned. And after her display here today, I just may change my plans for her also."

"If you do that – what I think you are thinking of anyway – it will cost you a lot of money."

"Not necessarily so Andy. I can always get someone else for that, but I think we may just have a gold mine in Mrs. Parker. We will certainly know by tomorrow night.

~~***~~

Damn it, Mary Jane thought when she entered the apartment. "The TV was on and that meant that Peter was home. She wasn't going to get a chance to 'lighten the load' so it looked like Petey was going to be getting it all. She was just going to have to tell him she was super horny that day plus being excited over being cast as the female lead in a movie. Well girl, you are an actress, let's go do it."

"Petey, Petey lover, I'm home."

"In the kitchen," her husband called back.

She ran into the kitchen and threw herself into his arms. "God baby, I'm so happy to see you. I've got great news Tiger; I'm going to star in a movie. Isn't that great? I'm just so excited that my pussy is dripping. Come on Tiger, I want dessert first tonight."

She took Peter by the hand and pulled him toward the bedroom. Peter, against his better judgement, and knowing full well the consequences of his confronting MJ about her having anything to do with Kraven was never the less getting ready to do just that. Mary Jane's excitement made him back down, at least until she settled down a little, and he followed along behind her to the bedroom. Mary Jane quickly stripped and threw herself down on the bed.

"Look at how wet I am Tiger. Thinking about what we did last night has had me horny all day and then the excitement of being cast in a movie, oh God Petey, I'm positively gushing. Come on Tiger, do what you do so well. Make me happy Tiger, make me happy."

It was at times like these that Peter really thanked that radioactive spider for having bitten him. Without that bite he would have been a normal man, not a super stud, and no way a normal man could have taken care of Mary Jane the way he could. Peter wondered if Mary Jane realized how lucky she was. Damn, she must have been real horny today. She was so wet that he could almost go swimming. Well, he knew what she loved and so he dove in.

Mary Jane was already building to an orgasm at just the thought of Spider-Man sucking up Kraven's special sauce and when Peter's tongue touched her pussy she cried out, "Oh yes Tiger, oh God yes" and images of Kraven's and Joe's big cocks danced in her head as her husband ate her pussy.

Chapter 5

At two in the morning, Peter left a softly snoring Mary Jane and went out for his nightly swing around the city. It was a pretty slow night considering. He interrupted a jewelry store robbery; two guys had broken the front window and were throwing the display merchandise in a bag when he webbed them and left them for the cops.

He left one man swinging upside down from a lamppost after catching the guy trying to boost a radio from a parked car.

And then he embarrassed himself. He saw three men in a bar parking lot and they had a woman bent forward over the trunk of a car. One man was thrusting into her and the other two were standing there watching and stroking their cocks while they waited their turn. At first Spidey didn't quite believe what he was seeing and he perched on the roof of the building next to the bar and took in the scene. The woman had her back to him, but Spidey did see that she had great legs and was wearing high heels and that had always been a big turn on for him. He was having a hard time believing that three guys would be doing this right out in the open where they could be seen and then he heard the women's voice, it was faint but he caught the "Don't" and a second later the "Please don't." Spidey knew then that she was being raped and he swung into action. In no time he had all three men webbed and on the ground and he turned to the woman.

"You are safe now. These animals are ready for the cops."

He barely got the words out of his mouth before the woman smacked him on the side of his head with her purse.

"You idiot!" she screamed, "I was almost there, he almost had me off."

"But I heard you; you said 'don't' and then I heard you say 'please don't."

"What I said you fucking shit head was "Don't stop, please don't stop.' Now you untie my husband and his brother's right this minute before I smack you in the head again."

Peter was shaking his head and as he swung away from the parking the woman was already bent back over the trunk of the car and screaming, "Fuck me, damn it, fuck me."

He decided to call it a night and go home.

~~***~~

It went pretty much as he had expected it would. He mentioned Kraven's criminal background, stated his belief that the man was a hardened criminal and was up to something and that Mary Jane should stay away from the man. Right on cue Mary Jane exploded.

~~***~~

"Your problem Peter is that you don't want me to have a career. You want me to stay at home and wait for you to decide to spend some time with me. When you aren't being Peter Parker, boy photographer, you are out web swinging and wall crawling while I sit here at home and stare at the walls and wait to hear that Spider-Man has finally been whacked by some super criminal or other. I'm not going to do it any more Peter. I will have a career and you can sit home waiting from now on," and then she flounced of to the bathroom and he heard the shower start running.

He picked up his fanny pack and checked to see that he had enough film in the camera and then he headed off to begin his day, as MJ had so quaintly put it, as a boy photographer.

~~***~~

Mary Jane was in her robe and drying her hair when the doorbell rang. She answered it and saw that it was Ralph, the owner of the apartment building.

"Morning Ralph. What brings you here? The rent isn't due for another week."

"I know Mary Jane, but I'm hurting. I haven't been laid in two weeks and I'm needing it bad."

"I'd like to help you out Ralph, you know I would, but this is just not a good time. I have rehearsals at nine and I'm already running late."

"Please MJ, just a quickie? Just let me take the edge off."

Mary Jane looked at the old, balding fat man and decided that she spare him enough time for a quick fuck. "Come on in Ralph. It will have to be a quick, no frills fuck. No head, no foreplay, just get it in and get it done."

"Thanks MJ, you're a peach."

"Come on in the bathroom with me Ralph. You can do me while I'm getting ready to go."

In the bathroom she took off her robe, spread her legs and leaned forward over the sink. She supported herself with one hand and said, "from behind Ralph, do me from behind."

As Ralph slid his cock into her, Mary Jane was using her other hand to brush her teeth and when that chore was done she picked up a hairbrush and started working on her long red hair.

"How you doing back there Ralph?"

"Almost there MJ, almost there."

Mary Jane usually enjoyed fucking Ralph, but today her career as a movie star was supposed to take off and quite frankly, she didn't have much thought for anything else. Ralph blew his nuts in her and she hardly noticed, but she did feel him pull out. She turned and bent to kiss him on his bald spot and said, "Sorry baby, I know it wasn't much fun for you, but I will make it up to you when you come back to collect the rent."

"That's okay MJ, I got off and that's what I needed."

Mary Jane walked him to the door and then hurried back to the bathroom to continue getting ready.

"We all set up and ready to go Andy?"

"Yes sir. The crew is standing by."

"What do you think Mrs. Parker's reaction is going to be?"

"I think she will go along with it right up to the point where she finds out what is really going on and then she will have a fit. You going to go all the way through with it?"

"I don't know yet Andy. It all depends on Mrs. Parker. If she responds like I hope she will, I will have to find another warm body so I can full fill the contract. If she doesn't respond well, today might be the end of it."

"I do hope she goes for it boss. I'd really like to have her around for a while."

"That makes two of us Andy."

~~***~~

Peter was one block from the apartment when his Spider Sense went off. He looked around just in time to see a car coming up over the curb and heading for him. He leaped to the side as the car roared past him and then took off down the street. Peter ducked into a hallway only to emerge seconds later as Spider-Man. He shot a stream of webbing up at a building and then swung up and began following the car that had tried to run him down.

"You can run sucka, but you can't get away from me."

Spidey followed the car halfway across town before the car pulled up and parked on a street down near the docks. As the driver got out of the car Spidey swung down and landed on the sidewalk in front of him.

"Anybody ever tell you that driving on the sidewalk is against the law?"

The man turned to run, but only got three steps before a strand of webbing stopped him.

"Hey dude, where you going? Have I got bad breath or something? Stick around – that's a joke son, sticky web holding you, get it? I want to talk with you about why you tried to run down my buddy Pete."

"I got nothing to say to you web-head."

"Oh sure you do. I'm a real likeable guy and I'm sure that a little conversation will show you that. Come on. Let's go to where we can be comfortable."

Two minutes later Spidey and the man were on the roof ledge of a twenty-five story building.

"What are we doing up here?"

"Having a private talk. You were about to tell me why you were trying to kill my buddy Peter Parker."

"No, I wasn't."

"Well then, I guess we can talk about something else."

"About what?"

"We can always talk about me. I like talking about myself. I'm a fascinating guy."

Spidey quickly webbed the man's feet and then lowered him over the ledge of the building, head down and hanging by a single strand of web.

"Sure you don't want to talk with me about why you were out to get Parker?"

"I ain't got nothing to say."

"Okay then, we can talk about me and some little known Spider-Man facts. Did you know that even though I can't leap tall buildings in a single bound I can climb the tallest building in town in less than a minute? I'm not faster than a speeding bullet either, but I am more powerful than a locomotive. You up on your Spider-Man lore? For instance, did you know that unless I use a catalyst my webbing deteriorates in about ten minutes? We are, what, twenty-five stories up? How about the fact that I didn't use catalyst on the webbing holding you to the side of the building. Did I mention that we are twenty-five stories up?"

"Let's see. You have been hanging there about three minutes now, seven or maybe a little less to go. Did you know that a falling body accelerates at one hundred and ten feet per second until it reaches terminal velocity? Let's see now, figuring eighteen feet per floor, twenty-five floors would be approximately four hundred and fifty feet so when the web breaks and you fall you should reach terminal velocity by what, the sixth floor? I could be a little off here – I never was much good at math – but the bottom line is that the Streets and Sanitation Department is not going to be happy with the mess they are going to have to clean up. Feel like talking to me yet?"

"You won't let me fall."

"I won't? Don't you read the Daily Bugle? J. Jonah Jameson calls me a threat to society, a menace to the citizens of this fair city. I mean hey, if you can't believe what you read in the papers, what can you believe? But what the heck, you don't want to talk I guess that's your business."

Spidey shot a strand of web to the building next door, looked at the man hanging there upside down and said, "see you down on the sidewalk" and got ready to swing off the ledge.

Suddenly the man said, "Wait, don't go. Don't leave me here."

"Talk to me, Bubba."

"It was a guy named Andy Zimmer what hired me to go after Parker."

"What about Kraven?"

"I don't know no Kraven. All I know is that Zimmer offered me five large to get rid of Parker."

"Where can I find this Zimmer?"

"He has an office somewhere in the warehouse district."

"Where are we going" Mary Jane asked. She had arrived at Kraven's office at eight forty-five and he had taken her right back down stairs to where the limousine was waiting.

"We are on the way to the sound stage, Mary Jane. We are going to start shooting the picture today."

"What about Brad?"

"We won't get to his scenes until next week."

"I haven't even seen a script yet."

"You'll have one to take home with you tonight. You won't need one for what we are going to shoot today. Today's stuff is mostly filler and without any structured dialog."

"Will Joe, Mark and Andy be there?"

Kraven smiled at her and said, "I'll see to it that you are taken care of, Mary Jane. In fact, we can start now," and he unzipped his trousers and took out his stiffening cock. Mary Jane eyed the large appendage jutting up from Kraven's lap and said, "don't mind if I do."

She lifted her skirt, pulled her thong off and then she straddled the big man. She used her left hand to brace herself against his shoulder as she used her right hand to guide his hard cock into her pussy. And as she sank down on it she said, "just what every girls dreams of; taking a ride while riding down Fifth Avenue."

~~***~~

When the limo pulled up at the warehouse, Kraven hit the button that lowered the partition that separated the front of the car from the back and then he looked in the back seat.

"Hurry it up Max, I've got a crew waiting inside and time is money."

"Sure boss," the chauffeur said as he slammed his black cock into Mary Jane's steaming wet box. "I'm almost there."

"Bring her inside when you're done."

"Sure boss," the dark brown driver said as Kraven exited the limo and entered the warehouse. Max was getting close and he pounded hard into the sexy redhead who was moaning, "oh yes, like that, fuck me hard baby" in his ear. Thank God the cunt carried condoms in her purse. He would have hated to miss out on the chance to fuck her while she was still relatively tight.

Since his juice was going to be going into a rubber anyway, he didn't bother to tell her he was coming; he just gave several hard pushes and then held himself still inside her as his cock spent itself. As he moved to get off her Mary Jane said, "you have a nice cock Max. Maybe we can do this again sometime."

Max smiled inwardly as he thought to himself, "a lot sooner than you think missy, and without that fucking raincoat."

Chapter 6

Mary Jane stood in the middle of the sound stage dressed in someone's idea of what a woman would wear on an African safari. Khaki shirt and shorts with way too many pockets and a pith helmet. Thick socks and hiking boots completed the outfit.

Several men, similarly attired, were lying on the floor with fake blood smeared on them. A mousy little man who had been introduced to her as the director made a motion and the AD (assistant director) shouted, "Places everyone." There was some stirring and then everyone was still.

"All right people, this is picture," the director said, "Roll camera."

A second later the soundman said, "speed," and the director pointed at Mary Jane and said, "Action!"

Mary Jane took a deep breath and then looked around her and wailed, "Oh my God, they're dead, they're all dead. I have to get out of here."

She turned to the left and started to go only to be stopped by the sight of three African warriors looking menacingly at her. She reversed course only to find four more in her path. Several of the black warriors leaped at her, grabbed her and pushed her to the ground as she screamed. Hands clutched at her clothes, ready to rip them off of her and she twisted and turned and screamed as she tried to fight them off. Suddenly the director hollered out, "Cut!"

He turned to Kraven and said, "this isn't going to work. The woman is just too damned sexy."

"What's the problem?"

"Look at my Africans, there isn't a soft dick among them and on film it is going to stick out like a sore thumb."

Kraven nodded and then said, "I have an idea." Turning to Mary Jane he said, "you can see the problem, right?" She nodded an amused yes. "I hate to bring this up and normally I wouldn't, but I saw you in action yesterday and I know that you have a strong sexual appetite." He motioned around him, "all this is costing a bundle and the quickest way to get back on track is to get rid of those stiff cocks. You are a professional Mary Jane and you have some idea of what production times cost. What do you think, can you help us out?"

Mary Jane looked over at the African warriors; Joe was one and so was Max. "Okay, I'll do it."

"Good girl. Can I ask a favor?"

"What?"

"You know what outtakes are, right?"

"Yes."

"As long as you are going to do it can I roll camera? I would like to film it for my own private library. I'd like to pick it up at the point where they wrestled you to the ground and have you act as if they are forcing you. After all, that was the purpose of the original scene. The only difference is that in the real movie Tarzan, played by Brad Pitt, he saves you before it happens. I'll even give an under the table, tax free bonus of say, twenty thousand?"

Mary Jane kicked and screamed and tried to fight them off, but they ignored her and ripped her clothes off her. "This would be Academy Award stuff if it was ever seen by the paying public," she thought as the last little wisp of clothing – her thong – was ripped off her.

She opened her mouth to scream again and a thick, dark chocolate cock was shoved in her mouth. Hands grabbed the back of her head and the cock started to fuck her face. A mouth attached itself to her right tit and fingers started pulling on her left nipple. More fingers entered her pussy and a thumb was pushed into her ass.

Her body tingled with that delicious "Fuck me" feeling that she loved so much, but the professional in her said, "Fight it off MJ, you are being forced here, play the part." She got one hand free and she beat on the chest of the warrior stuffing his cock in her mouth and she kept struggling and trying to break free of them. He legs were pushed apart and she felt the first slab of meat pierce her outer lips and it felt so damned good.

She moaned around the cock in her mouth as the cock in her pussy began to pound into her hard and fast. In the back of her mind she felt it rear its head, "Oh shit," she thought, "there goes my Academy Award" as her first orgasm washed over her. She felt the cock in her mouth throb and she knew it was only seconds away from pushing a load down her throat. At that exact instant she felt the cock in her pussy pulse and her insides were splashed by hot sperm.

"Oh my God!" her mind screamed at her, "They aren't wearing condoms!" and she really struggled and tried again to break free. Hands held her legs apart as another black warrior moved between them and pushed his hard lance deep into her. The cock in her mouth spit out it's offering and she was forced to swallow it all or choke. When the cock pulled out of her mouth she cried out, "No, please God no, you ca...." But another cock was shoved into her mouth before she could finish saying "do me without rubbers."

~~***~~

For the next several hours Mary Jane Parker was stuffed with cock as one man after another fucked her. She had stopped her struggles and her body welcomed the invaders. She had orgasm after orgasm as her legs wrapped around torsos and her fingers dug into butt cheeks. She screamed out in pleasure and begged the men to fuck her harder and make her cum.

Mary Jane had so many orgasms that her body was drained of strength and she was exhausted. She was so tired that when she was positioned on her hands and knees and Max took her anal virginity her scream of pain didn't have any more steam behind it than one of her low moans of pleasure (Peter had been there, but with him only having three inches it could still be considered untouched). By the time Max had emptied himself in her ass, the pain had subsided and she was pushing her butt back at him. Max pulled out of her ass and the other six Africans lined up to pooper poke her.

When the last of the black warriors had finished packing Mary Jane's fudge, Kraven made a signal to the cameraman and the camera was turned off. And then Mary Jane really got worked over as the rest of the cast and crew took turns ramming their cocks into whichever hole they fancied. Cameraman, soundman, gaffers, best boy, key grip, dolly grip and the janitor who kept the sound stage clean all fucked her. By the time the dead safari members got up off the floor and unzipped, Spider-Man's slut wife had passed out from exhaustion.

~~***~~

When she awoke Mary Jane's entire body hurt. She sat up and saw that she was on a small cot in a room with no windows. She got up and went to the door and found that it was locked. She started beating on the door and demanding to be let out. Nothing happened for several minutes and then the door opened and Kraven came in.

"Why am I in here? Why have you locked me up?"

"It was necessary to give me some time to figure out what to do with the Widow Parker."

"The Widow Parker? I don't understand."

"Right about now your husband should be stuffed into a trash can in some alley and the question for the Widow Parker is would she like to be in the next trash can over or would she rather be my own personal sex toy?"

"I still don't understand."

"It is simple Mary Jane. You are drop dead gorgeous and the most magnificent piece of ass I've ever had and it would be an absolute shame to have to kill you and stuff your body in a trash can somewhere. Hence the question, 'Would you rather be dead or my personal sex toy?'"

"I still don't understand what this is all about."

"It is about money Mary Jane, an awful lot of money. There is an extremely wealthy man who wants a one of a kind, one-copy only – his porno film. You know what a 'snuff film' is Mary Jane?"

"Oh my God!" Mary Jane moaned as she finally realized what Kraven was saying.

"God can't help you here Mrs. Parker, but I can. I'm being paid two million dollars for the film. You don't have to be the one snuffed. All my principal specified was that it should be a busty redhead."

"What is this stuff about the Widow Parker and Peter being stuffed in a trash can?"

"When you had died and we had disposed of your body, we couldn't have your husband looking for you, now could we. It was a tidy solution to a vexing problem. Everything is wrapped up nicely. Your husband would be dead, you would have disappeared and the police would start looking for you as the prime suspect. I mean you were obviously guilty or why had you run? And your husband is dead. Our man hasn't reported in yet, but Slasher is the best in the business. He has never failed."

The actress in Mary Jane took over as she suppressed the joy in her heart. Her Peter was alive! And as long as she was alive there was hope. She knew he was alive because there wasn't any way in the world that a man could get close enough to Petey to hurt him because of his Spider Sense. Oh no, if you wanted to take out her Tiger it would have to be from half a mile away with a pretty accurate sniper rifle. No, her baby was okay and all she had to do was stay alive until he found her. Kraven had wanted an actress, she would give him one.

"What are you, stupid? Come on Kravey baby, you've seen me in action. Do you think I'd really choose a trashcan over a cock like yours? Just tell me you aren't serious about my being your private sex toy. Don't tell me that you are going cut me off from Max, Joe, Mark, and yes, even little Andy. You have a super cock Kravey, but you've seen me sweetie, I need cock, a lot of cock."

Kraven chuckled, "I'll see to it you get all you want Mary Jane and I'm going to make you a star. It will be of porno films, but you will be a star."

Mary Jane giggled, "Well, that certainly should get me all the cock I want."

"Course, the down side for me is now I have to start all over on my snuff film."

"Not necessarily."

"What do you mean by that?"

"I know a girl who looks enough like me to be my double. Might have to play with camera angles a little, but we can off her and still use the footage of me."

"You're kidding. You would set up a friend?"

"She's not a friend, just someone that I know. And for a share of two million I would have snuffed my husband myself. Just make sure that you keep that film in a safe place so we won't have to waste money hiring another crew and re-shooting."

"I have the film safe in the warehouse office. Who is this woman we can use?"

"Her name is Mellisa Courtland. I'll give her a call and ask her to meet me for a drink and you can take it from there." Thank God she is in Denver MJ thought, it will buy me some time. Time for Petey to find me and rescue me; and time for me to find a way to destroy that film.

~~***~~

At that very minute, Spider-Man was moving from warehouse roof to warehouse roof looking for something that would indicate where he could find Andy Zimmer. He had covered almost all the warehouses in the district before he saw something that grabbed his interest. There was a limo parked outside one of the warehouses and it was a limo that he recognized. One look at the plate number showed him that it was the same limousine that had carried Kraven and MJ from Adolpho's to the hotel. He settled on the roof of the building and tried to make sense of what he knew. It could be a coincidence that this Andy Zimmer guy had an office in the warehouse district and Kraven's limo was parked at a warehouse in the warehouse district, but he didn't believe in coincidences where criminals like Kraven were concerned. No, Andy Zimmer must be one of Kraven's henchmen.

So why would Kraven want Peter Parker eliminated? Given that Kraven didn't know that Spider-Man and Peter Parker were one and the same the only tie between Kraven and Peter was MJ. What could Kraven want with Mary Jane that would require the removal of her husband? Well, he wasn't going to find the answer to that question sitting on a roof. He looked around for a skylight or some other way into the building.

In the office twenty-one feet below where Spidey was standing, Mary Jane was on her knees with Kraven's cock in her mouth. Standing just behind her and sliding his cock into her ass was the object of Spider-Man's search. Andy had missed the afternoon gangbang, but he didn't mind now that he knew the redheaded whore was going to be around for a while. Mary Jane was giving Kraven the best blow job she was capable of hoping that he would lean back and relax and not notice that she was checking out the room. She had located the two film cans, but she needed to find a way into the room and get them and then escape. She had no doubt that Peter would find her and save her, but that film had to be destroyed before there was any chance that he could see it.

Ideas were running rampant in her head and she was shooting most of them down as soon as they occurred to her as being improbable or impossible. Then she remembered seeing two gasoline cans sitting next to a portable generator on the sound stage. If they were full, or even half full, they would give her what she needed to start a nice fire. Open the film cans, pour gasoline on the film and then throw a match on the pile and that should take care of things. But she had to find a way to get to the film cans without being seen.

Her thoughts were interrupted as Andy's pounding into her butt hole brought on an orgasm and as her body shook Kraven grabbed the back of her head and punched a load down her throat. God, but she was going to miss the asshole when Peter got around to taking him down. He had the sweetest cum she had ever tasted and he was a great fuck. Too bad he was a criminal. Maybe she could fuck him a couple of more times before the curtain came down on him.

~~***~~

Peter Parker, in his guise as the Super Hero Spider-Man, checked out the skylight on the roof of the warehouse. It was locked on the inside, but a little Spider Strength was applied and he pulled the whole assembly loose from its mounting. It did make some noise though and Mark and Joe, who had been working on the sound stage, looked up to see where the noise came from. They saw Spider-Man swinging down as he said, "Hi guys. Can one of you tell me where I can find Andy Zimmer?"

Joe was just a little smarter and faster than Mark. Realizing that the web head could snare both of them with a web net if they were standing close together he broke to his left while at the same time drawing his gun. Mark, suddenly realizing the threat that the wall crawler presented, pulled out his gun and got off one wild shot before being entombed in webbing.

"I'll bet you guys don't get much company when you exhibit such anti-social behavior," Spidey said as he turned his attention to Joe.

"Die, you fucking insect!" Joe snarled as he pointed his gun at Spider-Man only to see his hand become encased in webbing before he could pull the trigger.

~~***~~

In the office, Kraven heard Mark's shot and he rushed to the door and looked out to see Spider-Man bundling Mark and Joe up in a cocoon of webbing. He turned back meaning to grab the film and Mary Jane, but then his instinct for survival kicked in and he yelled at Andy, "Let's get the fuck out of here!" and then he turned and ran for the door and the limousine waiting outside. Spidey turned and saw Kraven and another man just as they went out the warehouse door and he started after them.

Mary Jane, recognizing the situation as her best chance to destroy the film, peeked out the door just in time to see her husband go out the door after Kraven. She ran out into the warehouse and got one of the gas cans that was sitting next to the portable generator and then ran back into the office. She opened the film cans and dumped the film on the floor and the emptied the gasoline on top of it. She grabbed her purse and moved to the door. Once there she turned and tossed a lit match into the room and was rewarded with a loud "fuhwomp" and an instant flame covered floor.

She turned and headed for a side door. Just as she left the warehouse she saw Joe and Mark on the floor in the middle of the sound stage. Her eyes looked longingly at Joe as she thought, "Damn, but I am going to miss that big slab of meat between his legs" and then she turned and beat feet.

~~***~~

Kraven and Andy hopped in the limo and tapped the napping driver on the shoulder. "Get us the fuck out of here Max; Spider-Man is just behind us."

The limo had been sitting there with the motor running so Max could have the heater running so all he had to do was drop the shift lever into DRIVE and floor the gas pedal. The limo tore away from the warehouse and Spider-Man was just getting ready to go after it when he heard the loud "fuhwomp" and looked back to see the flickering flames through the warehouse windows.

He turned and started after Kraven and then he remembered the two men he had left tied up in the warehouse. "Shit," Peter said to himself, "Can't be a Super Hero without having some values. Even though they both would have shot me if they could have I can't just take off and leave them in a burning building."

He cast on last glance at the disappearing taillights of the fleeing limousine, "We will meet again asshole, count on it" and then he turned to go back into the burning warehouse.

~~***~~

Mary Jane stayed in the shadows as much as possible as she made her way through the warehouse district trying to get to an area where she could flag down a cab. She heard a car coming and she turned hoping to see the familiar bright yellow of a cab; instead she saw a limo coming and she ducked into a doorway and waited for it to speed on by.

"Damn," she thought, "that might have been Kraven and I damned sure don't want to see him again. I've got to find a cab and beat Petey home and get in the tub and soak. What a waste. As much jizz as I've had pumped into me today, I know I would really get off having Petey eat my pussy tonight, but I don't dare. My pussy and my asshole must look like the Holland Tunnel after all the meat that was stuffed into them today. I don't dare let Petey go down there and get a close look. Damn it, why can't you ever find a fucking cab in this town when you need one."

~~***~~

The apartment was strangely quiet when he entered it. "MJ, I'm home."

"In the bathroom, Tiger."

Peter walked into the bathroom and found Mary Jane soaking in the water-filled bathtub. "Hard day?" he asked.

"Very. It is hotter than hell being under all those bright lights and constantly being on your feet as you shoot scene after scene."

"Did you enjoy your brief stint at being a star?"

"Brief stint? What are you talking about?"

"Kraven's film studio burned to the ground a couple of hours ago and he's on the run from the law."

"What did he do?"

"It seems for some reason he wanted your husband dead and he hired a guy called the Slasher to do it."

"I suppose that now you will give me the 'I told you so' lecture?"

"I told you he was up to no good, Mary Jane, but would you listen to me?"

"Is that why you are in here Peter, to rub it in?"

Mary Jane saw the skin around Peter's eyes tighten as he clenched his jaw, turned and walked from the room and she knew she had accomplished what she wanted. He would pout for a day or two and avoid her and that would give her holes time to tighten up. She would make it up to him. He loved it when she sucked and licked his little pee pee and a couple of days of that and he would get over his mad.

Life just wasn't fair. She loved him so much and wanted him so bad and he was just so totally fucking worthless in bed. Damn good thing she had her list of lovers and tomorrow was Friday; time to go see Jameson and Robby again.

The End

Here is a preview of another story you may also enjoy:

Just Plain Bob

for *Too Hot*

HENRY

HOT ROMANCE EROTICA

I got up to go to the bathroom and I noticed that the bedside clock read 3:15. The light from the full moon was coming in the window and it showed her long blond hair fanned out across the pillow. She had kicked the sheet off and the little dangly thing that was pierced in her skin at the navel reflected the light of the moon across her flat stomach as if from a prism. I gazed at her clean shaven pubes and then at the half inch nipples on her 34D cup breasts and wondered how in the hell we had we ended up in bed together.

~~***~~

It started in the tenth grade when my assigned seat in English Composition was right next to Maxine Barber. Maxine, she preferred Maxi, was eighteen going on twenty-five and she wasted no time in letting the rest of us know that we were nowhere near being her equals. She hung with the seniors and was a cheerleader and that made her just so much better than the rest of us lowly sophomores.

Mrs. Harbauer was a no-nonsense teacher and as far as she was concerned, whatever she said in her classroom was 'law' and that was the name of that tune. We were halfway through the semester when she broke the class into teams of two and assigned each team a topic to research and do a seventy-five hundred word paper on. Lucky me, I was given Maxine as a partner. Maxine promptly protested being placed with me and Mrs. Harbauer promptly let Maxine know where the bear shit in the woods.

Well! You couldn't tell Maxine what to do so she solved the problem by not working with me at all which did not bother me in the least because Maxine's attitude toward her peers sucked and I didn't want anything to do with the bitch anyway. So I set off on my own, did the research and started on the paper. The paper was almost done when Maxine found out that the grade on the paper would count as sixty percent of the final grade for the course. No paper meant that Maxine would fail the class and that would lead to her being dropped from the cheerleading squad because of failure to maintain a 'C' average in all of her classes.

Suddenly Maxine decided that not all sophomores were losers and that I just happened to be one of the winners. She came to me and wanted to know what I wanted her to do as her part of the paper. I laughed at her and told her that her name would not be appearing on the paper. I told her that I had done all the work and the paper was three-quarters typed and she could kiss my ass and go back to running with the seniors. That kind of set her back on her heels. She was not used to being told no. She said a few unkind words about my parentage and stalked off.

The next day she was back apologizing and then she asked me what she could do to get her name on the paper.

"You don't have that much money Max."

"I don't like being called Max."

"Tough shit Max."

"Come on Henry, there must be something I can give you to put my name on the paper."

"I don't like being called Henry. I prefer Hank."

She was on the ragged edge of giving me back my "tough shit" when she caught herself.

"How about we go out on a date or two?"

I laughed.

"Come on Hen…Hank, help me out here."

"I have no reason to help you Max."

"Would a couple of hand jobs change your mind?"

I laughed at her again. "You can't be serious Max. I can do that for myself."

"Can you give yourself a blow job?"

"No, but so what?"

"How about head for my name on the paper?"

I did not want to put Maxine's name on the paper, but I wasn't stupid. I was like every other guy my age – I wanted sex! I was not a virgin – hadn't been for two years – but pussy wasn't all that easy to come by when you were eighteen. I'd gotten some, but not near as much as I would have liked. Maxine wanted her name on the paper? I'd just have to find out how bad.

"A blow job won't do it, Max. The price is two dates with you to take place on the two days prior to when the paper is due."

Her face lit up and then I gave her the rest of it. "And on both of those dates you will suck my cock and give me your pussy and your ass."

"No fucking way!"

To purchase the book, look for **<u>Too Hot for Henry</u>**.

Here is another preview of a story you may enjoy:

BBW
LOST & FOUND
THE CRUISE SERIES, BOOK 1

JESSICA JOHANNSEN

If Belinda weren't staring right at it, she never would have believed that it could be true. As Belinda peered down at the computer screen, the woman in the photo seemed to stare right back. The woman's casual grin made Belinda feel mocked; made her feel as though the woman flaunted what she possessed.

Belinda covered her mouth with both hands to contain the scream that built in her throat. The young, sexy blond was her husband's mistress; the pictures on his computer finally answered the question that she had been too afraid to ask. No, it wasn't her imagination; their marriage of fifteen years had finally passed the point of no return.

She knew she had to finish getting ready for work. Sitting here at her husband's desk, wearing only a bra and skirt, she felt open, exposed, and raw.

Belinda searched the contents of her husband's hard drive, finding album after album of photos. There were hundreds of pictures of the mistress, in every state of dress and undress. Skipping back to the earliest album, she checked the upload date. Her stomach lurched when she realized that the first pictures were dated over a year ago. Almost to the day that her husband had moved out of their bedroom and taken up permanent residence in the den.

Belinda wound her long black hair up into the bun that she wore for work. She applied make-up. She puckered and blew a kiss to her reflection, a silly habit. She flinched, realizing that many of the photos her husband kept were pictures of the blond woman making just that face, the wink and kiss.

Tears threatened to fall. She closed her eyes and took a deep breath. He had already ruined their marriage; she would not let him ruin her meeting with the board. Belinda turned her mind to work, making sure she arrived in the conference room before anyone else. She set about preparing the screen.

When Mr. Whiting entered the room, she was standing at the podium, reviewing the presentation in her mind. His presence had always unnerved her; she had forgotten that he'd be there this morning until this moment. He nodded at her as he made his way to the back of the room.

"Belinda, are you ready?" he asked.

"As ready as I'll ever be," she said.

She regretted how it had sounded, so unsure of herself. It wasn't fair that the blond got her husband and her self-confidence all in one fell swoop.

"You'll be great," he assured her.

Mr. Whiting always undressed her with his eyes. Today was no different; she could feel his gaze peeling away the layers of her clothes.

Tall, broad-shouldered, with blond hair and piercing blue eyes, Robert Whiting was considered quite a catch. Belinda had entertained dirty thoughts about him a time or two, turned more than once to catch a glimpse of his backside as he passed. She always shook her head and reproached herself. She was a married woman; she didn't drool over men.

Today, though… she could drool all she wanted, over anyone that caught her eye. Mr. Whiting just happened to be foremost in her mind when it came to hot, single men.

Belinda ran her hands down her waist and her round hips, feeling nervous. She checked her watch. Everyone else would be arriving shortly and she couldn't help but wonder if Mr. Whiting hadn't gotten here early just to get her alone.

In her mind's eye, she imagined sauntering towards him, returning that lustful gaze. Sliding down into his lap, feeling her skirt rise on her thighs. Exposing her garters and stockings, pressing herself against what she imagined was an impressive erection. She would lick her lips as she ran her hand slowly down the front of his pants, longing to unzip them so badly and wrap her dainty fingers around his manhood.

A loud sigh escaped her lips. She flushed, embarrassed. Perspiration teased the back of her neck; her blouse was damp.

This was ridiculous, but she couldn't help it. She added this moment of embarrassment to her husband's lengthy list of crimes. Cut off from sex for a year, Belinda was so needy that she was ready to risk it all to bump and grind in the boardroom. More than that, Mr. Whiting was her boss, and far too young for her. She gave herself a sharp reprimand for her unacceptable behavior, pulling herself together…

If you enjoyed this sample then look for **BBW Lost and Found**.

Also by this Author:

The Prodigal Family: The Abbotts

Watching My Shared Wife

The Waitress and the Runaway Husband

Baiting Mr. Little

Too Hot for Henry

From the Author

If you enjoyed any of my books then please share the love and promote my books in Amazon.

If you write me a review and send me an email I will send you a free book, or many.
(Just know that these emails are filtered by my publisher.)

Good news is always welcome.

One Last Thing, For Kindle Readers...

When you turn the page, Kindle will give you the opportunity to rate this book and share your thoughts on Facebook and Twitter. If you enjoyed my writings, would you please take a few seconds to let your friends know about it? Because... when they enjoy they will be grateful to you and so will I.

Thank You!

An Open Letter from Just Plain Bob

A message for those who like my stories, those who hate my stories, those who are indifferent and those who have yet to make up their minds.

I have often stated that I really don't care what others think about my stories, that I write for my own enjoyment and then I offer to share. If you like my stories fine and if you don't, also fine since I have already satisfied my target audience - me!

It is human nature to strive to get better. If you take up bowling your first games are going low scoring, but you will work and practice to get better and as your average climbs you may forget the game where you had three gutter balls and shot an eighty-six, but that game is still there in your past.

Your first time on the golf course you shot an eighty on the front nine, but did you settle for that being your game or did you work to improve? You may eventually get a three handicap, but that nine hole eighty is still there as part of your past.

When you hired in at your job did you say, "Cool, I got it made" and do nothing more than what you barely had to do or did you go to work thinking that, "Someday I'm going to be running this place." You might never climb that high, but human nature says that you are going to at least try.

It is the same with authors who write stories and post them on sites like Literotica. Their first stories might not be all that good, but comments and feedback along with a desire to get better drive them toward putting out a better product or to at least try.

I'm no different. My first stories might not have been all that great, but they are still there on the hard drive. I like cheating wife stories and five years ago I found my first adult site that catered to cheating wife stories. It was a pay site, but it had a policy of giving a free lifetime membership to anyone who submitted five stories to the site. How hard can that be I said to myself as I sat down and fired up the word processor and went to work.

I sent my five stories in and sat back to enjoy my free membership and a funny thing happened. I started getting feedback, most of it positive, and I became hooked. I started cranking out more stories. The site I was sending my stories to had seven categories:

Bisexual
Cream Pie
Groups

I Watch
Gang Bang
Racial
SM/BD

I know nothing about bisexual or SM/BD and I had no interest in Groups so all the stories I wrote I tailored for the four remaining categories:

Cream Pie
I Watch
Gang Bang
Racial.

I turned out eight stories a month, two for each category, which means that after five years I have over 120 stories in each of those categories and they are all still on the hard drive.

A year ago I received an email asking me why I never posted stories on Literotica. The answer? I didn't know about Lit. I pulled it up, liked what I saw, and started sending in stories to it. All new stories? No, not hardly, not with over 400 stories sitting on the hard drive. Maybe one new story for each fifteen or so old ones. The newer ones are better, at least I think they are and I have received some feedback that leads me to believe that others think so too, and I will continue to write new ones.

But I am still going to recycle what is on the hard drive, stories that were written specifically to fit the four categories. That means that those of you who hate cream pie stories still have eighty or so to look forward to. Ditto for those who call me a racist; you will get another seventy or so interracial stories.

Those who hate wimps will only see about fifty more of those because the stories I sent to the I Watch category were split 50/50 between what some call wimps and some call "real men." Why the 50/50 split? It came from listening to the readers. I would get feedback asking me why all the men in my stories were hard asses. "In real life men are more forgiving, especially if it is the first indiscretion." So I would write stories with forgiving husbands and boyfriends and then the next batch of feedback would say, "Why are all your husbands spineless wimps" and I'd write stories that went back the other way.

Eventually I came to realize that I was wasting my time - there was no way I could write a story that would satisfy everybody and that is when I adopted my philosophy of writing for my own enjoyment and then offering to share.

As far as the gangbang stories? Well, what can I say? Gangbangs are gangbangs and there are still eighty or so of them to go.

The bottom line is that Literotica readers are going to see more of my old stories than my new ones. If I'm still around three or four years from now it will probably go the other way, more new than old.

I feel the need to respond to some of the comments and emails I have received. By far the largest percentage comes from people who say, "You are an asshole because all women are not whores and sluts and that's all you make them out to be."

Next most common is, "You must really hate women you sick fuck."

"You must be a wimp because all the men in your stories are wimps" is up there in the top ten along with, "Why don't you give it a rest and go crawl off in a hole somewhere."

There is a lot more, but I'm only going to address those four and in reverse order.

I won't stop and go crawl in a hole because I am enjoying the hell out of what I am doing and remember what I said, I am doing this for MY OWN ENJOYMENT and then I offer to share. Some obviously like my sharing with them and so I will continue to do so. No one is holding a gun to a reader's head and telling them they must click on a Just Plain Bob story or die. It is a conscious choice on the reader's part to move that mouse and click on that story.

When a man finds out he has a cheating wife or girlfriend there are only a limited number of ways he can handle it. If he loves her he can forgive, try to forget and try to hold on and somehow make things work. He can turn his back on her, walk away and get on with his life. The third option is to take revenge.

According to a good portion of those who send me feedback the first and second options are proof that the men are wimps. If the man takes the third option he is still considered a wimp if he doesn't do some sort of physical damage to the woman and her lover. These readers believe that the only way not to be a wimp is to kill, maim and destroy everything in sight. Doing that however, will invariably get the man throw in jail and that is why it so rarely happens in real life.

In real life most revenge takes place in the man's head when he says to himself, "I should have _____ (fill in the blank) the fucking cunt!" I know this because I have been there and done that (see The Dark Trilogy). In my stories I try to mirror real life so kill, maim and destroy are going to be for the most part absent. Outside of some fisticuffs there will be very little physical violence in my stories. Most of my husbands are going to do what I did, what several of my friends and others that I know have done, forgive, or walk away. If this makes them wimps and me a wimp for writing the story that way, so be it.

Next is the "I must hate all women." Nothing could be farther from the truth. I love women. I lust after women. I even like whores and sluts. I have been married four times, engaged two other times (that did not end in marriage) and I have always had girlfriends between marriages. My philosophy is that women were put on this earth for me to enjoy and I'm not talking just sexually. I could sit at the mall (and have) for hours and just girl watch.

The engagements, girlfriends and three of the four marriages bring me to the #1 anti JPB comment on the list.

"You are an asshole because all women aren't whores and sluts."

Well dear reader, you can not prove that by me! I will say up front that I KNOW all women aren't whores and sluts, BUT the majority of the women in my life were. My mother ran around on my father for years while he was driving a truck for a living. My Aunt Margaret cheated regularly on my Uncle Bill, as did my Aunt Mildred on my Uncle Paul. My Aunt Betty fucked around on my Uncle Bob for years and finally left him for his brother, my Uncle Wendell. Uncle Wendell in turn caught her on her knees at his company Christmas party giving Season's Greetings to his boss.

My sister is three times divorced and each divorce came about when the then current husband caught her out spreading pollen. Both of the engagements I mentioned ended when I found out that I was not the one and only and a lot of the girls I dated between marriages never made it to engagement status for the same reason.

And that brings me to my three ex-wives. The first one, Helen (I believe I commented on her in the intro to The Dark Trilogy) had seven different lovers before I found out what was going on. I was living proof that love is blind. Ditto with my second wife. She had a secret life that she hid from me and when I found out about her brother, his friends and the gangbangs she was history.

My third marriage ended in divorce because of a different kind of cheating (and I can just imagine the outrage I am going to get over this) - she cheated on me with an idea. I was away from home on business, she was lonely, a couple of Jehovah's Witnesses knocked on the door and my wife, with nothing better to do invited them in. When I came home from my trip I found out that she had found God. On a scale that runs from TRUE BELIEVER on one end to ATHEIST on the other you will find me just to the right of AGNOSTIC and since I would not allow myself to be SAVED the marriage eventually died.

So yes, I write about sluts and whores because as everyone knows, you tend to write about the things you know. And I do like sluts and whores, just not the ones that lie to me and cheat on me.

So be forewarned - if you click on a Just Plain Bob story you will be getting sluts, whores and husbands who do not kill, maim and destroy. There are other things you will rarely find in a Just Plain Bob story. Even though I try to mirror real life my stories all take place in StoryLand. In StoryLand STDs and unwanted pregnancies do not exist unless the author feels like they may add something to the story. Bad things do not happen in StoryLand unless the author so wills it and no amount of "You should have..." in comments and feedback will change a story already posted.

Lastly, I will touch on a truth. None of what I have written here means shit because the same readers will still read the same stories that they profess to hate and make the same comments they have always made. Knowing this, I will deliberately post stories that will have them frothing at the mouth.

It is the least I can do for an adoring public.

Thank you!

Just Plain Bob
justplainbob@awesomeauthors.org

www.ingramcontent.com/pod-product-compliance
Lightning Source LLC
Chambersburg PA
CBHW071340130626
46556CB00004B/1963